Sharing Books From Birth to Five

Welcome to Practical Parenting Books

It's never too early to introduce a child to books. It's wonderful to see your baby gazing intently at a cloth book; your toddler poring over a favourite picture; or your older child listening quietly to a story. And you are your child's favourite storyteller, so have fun together while you're reading – use silly voices, linger over the pictures and leave pauses for joining in.

In *Baby Friends Come to Play*, a group of mums and babies get together for a morning's fun. Enjoy the nursery-rhyme rhythm of the words and ask your child to point to the toys as you name them. In each room, lift the flap to find out which Baby Friend is hiding, and see if you can you spot the little penguin!

Books open doors to other worlds, so take a few minutes out of your busy day to cuddle up close and lose yourselves in a story. Your child will love it – and so will you.

Jane & Clare

Jane Kemp   Clare Walters

P.S. Look out, too, for *Busy Babies Go to the Gym*, *Busy Babies Go Swimming* and *Busy Babies Go to the Play Club,* the companion books in this age range, and all the other great books in the Practical Parenting™ series.

AGE
1-2

Meet the Baby Friends

Ella Ben Matt Kate Charlie

First published in Great Britain by HarperCollins*Publishers* Ltd in 2001

1 3 5 7 9 8 6 4 2

ISBN: 0-00-664783-9

Practical Parenting™ is an IPC trademark © IPC Media 2001
Text copyright © Jane Kemp and Clare Walters 2001
Illustrations copyright © Jonathan Langley 2001

The Practical Parenting™/HarperCollins pre-school book series has been created by Jane Kemp and Clare Walters.
The Practical Parenting™ imprimatur is used with permission by IPC Media.

The HarperCollins website address is: www.**fire**and**wate**r.com

Manufactured in China

Practical Parenting™ is published monthly by IPC Media.
To get Practical Parenting™ delivered to your door every month ring the subscriptions
hotline on 01444 445555 or the credit card hotline (UK orders only) on 01622 778778.

Baby Friends
Come to Play

Written by Jane Kemp and Clare Walters
Illustrated by Jonathan Langley

Collins
An imprint of HarperCollins*Publishers*

Hello! We're the Baby Friends
Rushing in to play.
Come inside and join our games
Around the house today.

Who's hiding behind the coats?

Bricks and books and teddies too,
Dolls for us to dress.
We love playing with the toys
And always make a mess!

Who's missing? Can you guess?

Giggling, wriggling, here we are
In our den upstairs.
Can you see us sharing cake
And pouring tea for bears?

Has anyone seen Ella?

Splish and splash! This water's fun,
We can make things float.
Mum's not sure, she says 'No more!'
And takes away our boat.

Where can Charlie be?

We're all tired and thirsty now,
Ready for a snack.
Slurp and burp, and crunch and munch,
We've finished the whole pack!

Who's found a funny hat?

Now it's time to wave bye-bye,
'See you soon,' we say.
Baby Friends have had such fun,
It's been a lovely day!

Sharing Books From Birth to Five

AGE 0–1

AGE 1–2

AGE 2–3

AGE 3–5

ALL £3.99

The Practical Parenting™ books are available from all good bookshops and can be ordered direct from HarperCollins Publishers by ringing 0141 7723200 and through the HarperCollins website: www.fireandwater.com

You can also order any of these titles, with free post and packaging, from the Practical Parenting™ Bookshop on 01326 569339 or send your cheque or postal order together with your name and address to: Practical Parenting™ Bookshop, Freepost, PO Box 11, Falmouth, TR10 9EN.